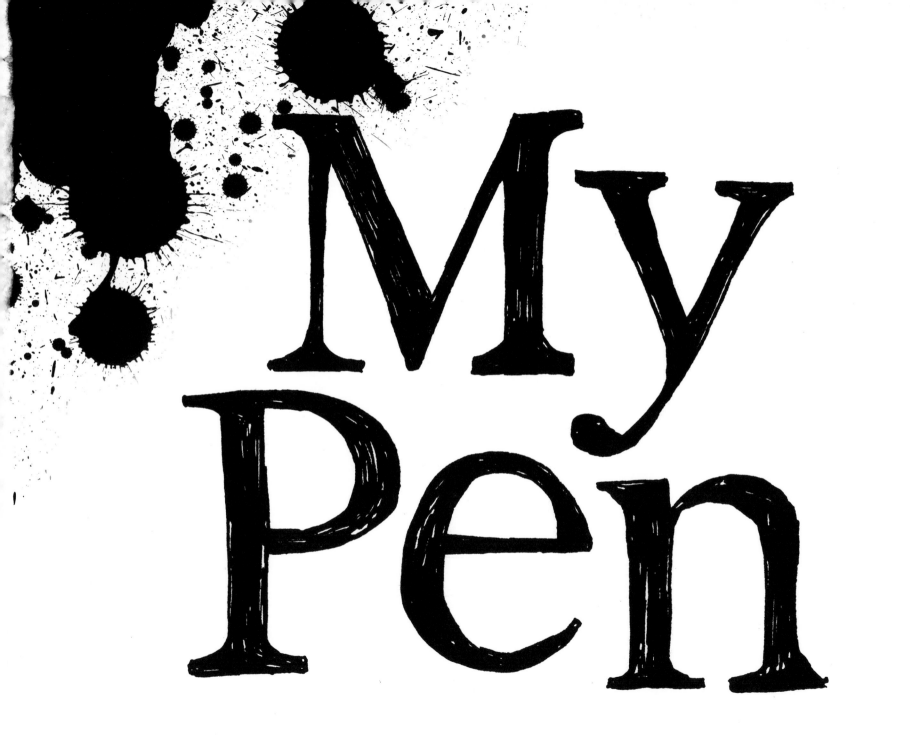

My
Pen

• Little, Brown and Company • Hachette Book Group • 1290 Avenue of the Americas, New York, NY 10104 • Visit us at LBYR.com • Originally published in hardcover by Disney • Hyperion, an imprint of Disney Book Group, in March 2015 • First Edition: March 2015 • Little, Brown and Company is a division of Hachette Book Group, Inc. The Little, Brown name and logo are trademarks of Hachette Book Group, Inc. • The publisher is not responsible for websites (or their content) that are not owned by the publisher. • Library of Congress Cataloging-in-Publication Data • Myers, Christopher, author, illustrator. • My pen / Christopher Myers.—First edition. • pages cm • Summary: An artist celebrates the many things he can do with a simple pen, and encourages the reader to do the same. • ISBN-13: 978-1-4231-0371-4 • ISBN-10: 1-4231-0371-8 • [1. Pens—Fiction. 2. Drawing—Fiction. 3. Imagination—Fiction.] I. Title. • PZ7. M9825My 2015 • [E]—dc23 • 2013047312 • ISBN 978-1-4231-0371-4 • PRINTED IN CHINA • APS • 10 9 8 7 6 5

My Pen

CHRISTOPHER MYERS

LITTLE, BROWN AND COMPANY

New York   Boston

THERE ARE RICH PEOPLE WHO OWN JEWELS AND
HOUSES AND PIECES OF THE SKY.

THERE ARE FAMOUS PEOPLE——MUSICIANS, ATHLETES,
POLITICIANS——WHOSE WORDS AND ACTIONS
SPREAD ACROSS TELEVISIONS AND NEWSPAPERS TO
EVERY EAR AND EYE ACROSS THE WORLD.

SOMETIMES I FEEL SMALL WHEN I SEE THOSE RICH
AND FAMOUS PEOPLE.

BUT THEN I REMEMBER I HAVE MY PEN.

MY PEN MAKES GIANTS OF OLD MEN

WHO HAVE SEEN BETTER DAYS.

THEN MY PEN PUTS THESE GIANTS

IN THE WARM, SWEET HANDS

OF THE SMALLEST GIRL.

MY PEN TAP-DANCES ON THE SKY

AND DRAWS CLOUDS WITH ITS FEET.

MY PEN

RIDES DINOSAURS

AND HIDES

AN ELEPHANT

IN A

TEACUP.

THEN MY PEN SAILS TO AFRICA

IN A NEWSPAPER BOAT.

AND

WEARS SATELLITE SNEAKERS

WITH COMPUTER LACES.

MY PEN HAS X-RAY VISION.

IT IS NOT 3D, BUT IT

WISHES THAT IT WAS.

MY PEN WORRIES ABOUT ALL THE WARS IN THE WORLD,

THEN TELLS EVERYONE I LOVE
THAT I LOVE THEM.

MY PEN IS SIMPLE AS A RAINDROP.

IT DRAWS ME A NEW FACE EVERY MORNING.

MY PEN TELLS STORIES IN THE MARGINS OF THE PAGE,

BUT IT DOESN'T ALWAYS
GET IT RIGHT.

SOMETIMES I CAN'T FIND MY PEN

(I THINK IT HIDES FROM ME).

BUT I KNOW MY PEN
CAN DO ANYTHING,
ANYWHERE.

THERE ARE A MILLION PENS IN THE WORLD
AND EACH ONE HAS A MILLION WORLDS INSIDE IT.

SO IF YOU HAVE A PEN, SEE WHAT YOU CAN DO—
LET THOSE WORLDS INSIDE YOUR PEN OUT!

To the people who make things,
and to the people who share them